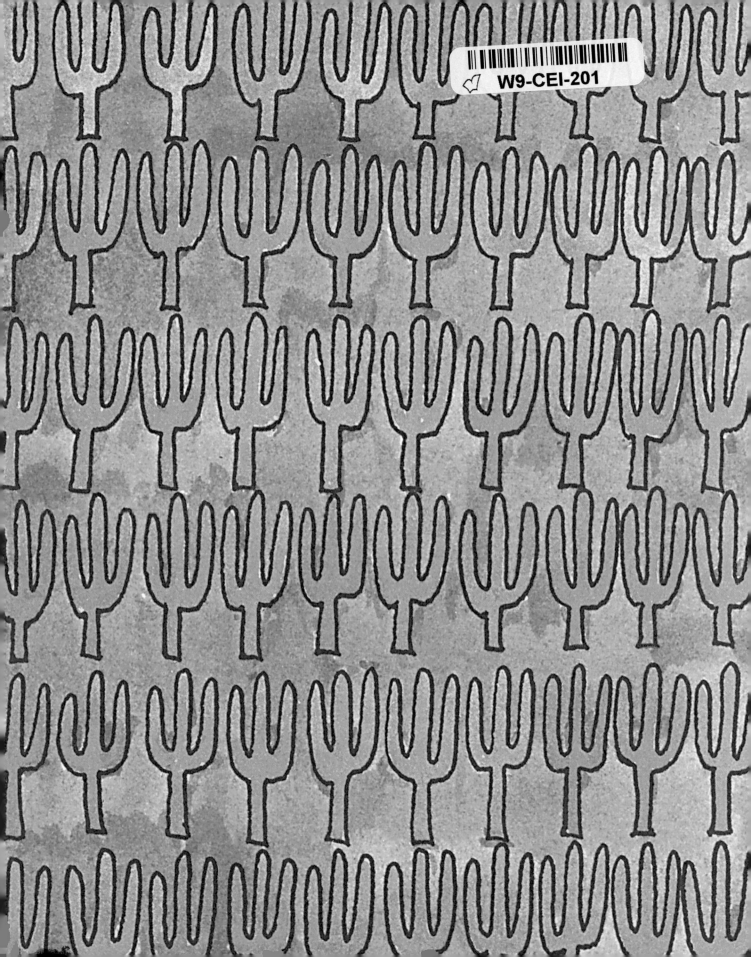

HENRY
GOES WEST

A HENRY DUCK BOOK

ROBERT QUACKENBUSH

ALADDIN   NEW YORK   LONDON   TORONTO   SYDNEY   NEW DELHI

FOR PIET, AND NOW FOR EMMA AND AIDAN

❦ ALADDIN
An imprint of Simon & Schuster Children's Publishing Division
1230 Avenue of the Americas, New York, New York 10020
This Aladdin hardcover edition November 2018
Copyright © 1982 by Robert Quackenbush
For information about special discounts for bulk purchases, please contact
Simon & Schuster Special Sales at 1-866-506-1949 or business@simonandschuster.com.
The Simon & Schuster Speakers Bureau can bring authors to your live event. For more
information or to book an event contact the Simon & Schuster Speakers Bureau
at 1-866-248-3049 or visit our website at www.simonspeakers.com.
Book designed by Nina Simoneaux & Tiara Iandiorio
The illustrations for this book were rendered in watercolor, pen, and ink.
The text of this book was set in Neutraface Slab Text.
Manufactured in China 0918 SCP
10 9 8 7 6 5 4 3 2 1
Library of Congress Control Number 2018944248
ISBN 978-1-5344-1537-9 (hc)
ISBN 978-1-5344-1539-3 (eBook)

HENRY THE DUCK missed his friend Clara, who was vacationing out west. He decided to pay her a surprise visit. So he packed his bag and took the first plane heading west to meet her.

Henry arrived at Clara's guest ranch early the next morning. But the ranch was closed. Everyone had just left for an all-day trail ride. They would not be back until midnight.

Henry decided to have a look around the ranch while he waited for Clara. As he was snapping a picture near the barn, Henry backed right into a mule.

The surprised mule kicked
Henry! Henry landed on the
back of a horse.

The horse was a bucking bronco!

Henry was taken for a wild ride.

Then he was tossed over a fence.

Henry landed in a bull's pen!

The bull chased Henry. Henry

ran and ran.

At last Henry got out of the bull's pen. He went to sit on a large rock. But he did not see the cactus behind it. Henry sat down on the cactus!

Henry jumped up and quacked
loudly. The noise frightened
some cattle grazing nearby.

The cattle began running.
Soon they were racing at full
speed. Henry had started a
stampede!

Henry escaped to the hills in the nick of time. He pulled the cactus stickers from his tail. Then he headed back to the ranch.

On the way, Henry spotted an unusual rock. He thought it would make a good present for Clara. But as soon as he picked up the rock . . .

He heard a loud rumbling from the mountaintop. Henry had started a landslide! He ran as fast as he could go.

Henry got clear of the landslide.

Then he went straight back to

the ranch to wait for Clara.

Henry waited and waited.

It was turning cold in the desert.

So Henry built a campfire.

He stood close to the fire to

warm his tail feathers. Too close.

Suddenly Henry's tail feathers began to sizzle! He made a beeline for the water and dove in.

Henry was soaking wet and
all worn out. He wished Clara
would hurry up and get there.

At last the riding party returned.

But Clara was not with them.

Henry asked one of the cowboys

if he had seen her.

"Sorry, mister," said the

cowboy . . .

"Clara went home yesterday.
She said she was lonesome for
someone named Henry."

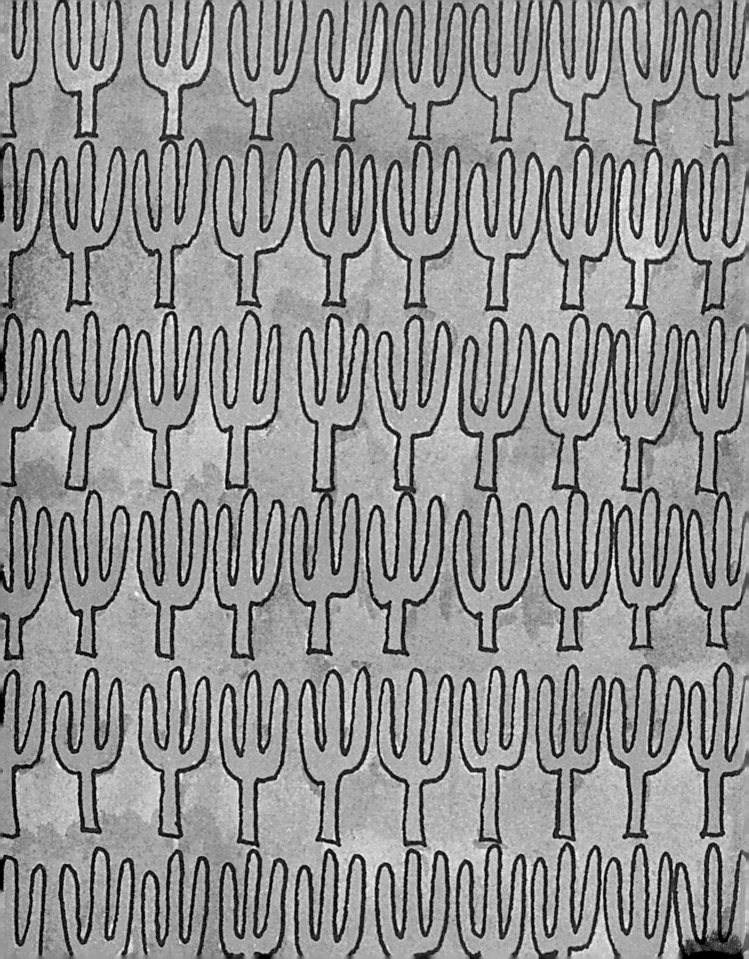